Maya's Voice

WRITTEN AND ILLUSTRATED BY
WEN-WEN CHENG

To my husband, whose love and encouragement kept me going.

To my little girls, who fill my heart with joy, laughter, and stories.

thanks big sis!

Maya had the sweetest voice that
she LOVED to share.

She chattered on and on with Mommy
about her love for red-pink.

She asked a zillion WHY questions while riding the bike with Daddy.

She hee-hawed with Sister
at the petting zoo.

She and her dollies yodeled high and low in preparation for their opening act.

One autumn day,
Maya started school.

Maya drew girl monsters
with curly eye lashes.

She wiggled and boogied
to the silliest tunes.

She clickety-clacked around
in sparkly princess heels.

She did all this at school without
her sweet voice.

The kids asked the teachers,
"Why doesn't Maya talk?"

The teacher asked Mommy,
"Does Maya talk at home?"

Her friends started speaking for her
when questions were asked.

Her carpet buddy pinched her.
She knew Maya wouldn't tell.

The next morning, Maya asked Mommy,
"Mama, can I stay home with you?"

With time, Maya's friends and teachers grew to understand and respect her quiet ways.

Then one spring day, Maya whispered
something soft. Her friend
overheard her and gave her a big hug.

He ran to the teacher and shouted,
"Maya's voice is cute!"

The next days and weeks after,
Maya's sweet voice grew and grew.

Maya's head nods and shakes
turned to murmurs of *yeses* and *nos*.

Her smile blossomed more and more as she played beside her friends.

Her teachers and friends cheered her on
in a patient and thoughtful way.

Then one remarkable day, she spoke to her friend like it was no big deal.

In the days that followed, Maya played house with her friends for the first time and loved it.

Maya's sweet voice was always there to share.
She was simply waiting for the moment
that was right for her.

Selective Mutism (SM) is a childhood anxiety disorder that is characterized by a child's inability to speak in public settings, such as school, despite speaking fully at home. Children with SM are often perceived as being shy, rude, or defiant and seldom receive the support they need to overcome the anxiety. SM is not something that children outgrow and early intervention is crucial. Without the proper help, SM can lead to future social and emotional problems.

One of our two girls experienced SM during her first years in preschool. It was heartbreaking to see her off each morning, knowing that she was likely not going to utter a single sound until Mommy or Daddy picked her up at the end of the day. Because of our lack of awareness of SM, we resorted to reasoning with her and reward systems to encourage her to speak. After many months of preschool with no progress, her preschool friends began to take notice and question why she did not speak. The more everyone questioned her or encouraged her to speak, the more anxiety she expressed about going to school. At this point, we knew we needed to seek help.

After a lot of late night research, we were relieved to find literature describing our child's experience called SM. We sought advice from professional psychologists and devised a plan to help our child. We met with the preschool director and her teachers and together discussed the first steps. They included ways to alleviate the pressure for Maya to speak as well as ways to divert her preschool friends' conversations from "Maya doesn't talk" to "Maya does talk and will when she is ready." Over the course of the year, we regularly checked in with the teachers to discuss her progress and next steps. Our top priority was always to make sure she had the opportunity, but felt no pressure, to speak. The process of supporting her speech in the classroom began with group songs and movements. When Maya felt more comfortable with nonverbal forms of expression, the teachers moved to asking simple "yes/no" questions. Gauging her readiness along the way, the teachers eased into close-ended choices like "Which cupcake flavor would you like?" and gradually transitioned into increasingly more open-ended prompts. It was a long and difficult journey with much heartache, but the dedicated and patient teachers worked with our family to help our little one through it.

That first year ended with a very special moment between Maya and one of her preschool teachers. Sitting on her teacher's lap, looking at her "Show & Tell" family poster that had been left unshared on the wall all year but was now removed and sorted in the "Home" pile, Maya began to speak. She pointed and described all the photos of her and her sister playing dress up, going on camping & biking adventures, hugging & kissing, and making silly animal faces at the zoo. It was the first time they shared a conversation together. Teary eyed, her teacher and I held our breath and listened to her sweet voice.
It was a beautiful moment that let us know that Maya was going
to be just fine.

It is our hope that, through our story, we can bring awareness, understanding, and support to children who suffer from Selective Mutism. Special thanks to all of Maya's preschool teachers and friends for all the love and patience!